To Patricia

I hope you enjoy this book as much as I enjoyed writing it.

Love

Shirley

Everyone Has A Story
(What's Yours?)

Oasis Publishing and Distribution

ISBN: 0-6154-8172-8
ISBN-13: 9780615481722

Everyone Has A Story
(What's Yours?)

Dr. Shirley Harmon

2011

Table of Content

Special thanks to
my husband and two sons.
Your encouragement and support
meant more than you will ever know.

Dear Diary

Dear Diary,

My parents are so lame. Once again, they are treating me like I am a baby. I am fourteen years old, but they want me to remain a little girl forever. I had plans to go to the mall and hang out with a couple of my friends, but my parents made other plans for me. Tonight they wanted me to eat dinner with the two of them and the most annoying little brother in the whole world. And it wasn't like mom actually cooked; she just picked up some food from the deli a few of blocks from the house. She bought a lemon-pepper rotisserie chicken. She knows I hate lemon pepper. I think she did it to make my life even more miserable. The green beans were overcooked and the rice was crunchy. Rice is not supposed to be crunchy. The best thing about the entire meal was the red fruit punch that came in a plastic gallon jug.

My dad was actually on time for dinner. What a surprise. Usually, he comes home late, so we never eat as a family except on special occasions like Thanksgiving or Christmas. Most of the time he tells mom he ate something at the office. Sometimes he comes home so late; I have already gone to bed and don't get to see him until the next morning. But for some reason today, he was on time, and he helped to set the table. Let me repeat that, Diary: he helped set the table. That task is usually reserved for my obnoxious little brother. My dad placed the plates on the table while Jay placed the silverware and napkins beside the plates. They were working together, as a team, and Jay was so happy he was laughing and smiling the entire time. Yeah, he is a brat, but it was nice to see him happy, and plus as long as my dad had him occupied that meant he was not bothering me or any of my stuff.

I know he is not the worst five-year-old in the world, but he is pretty close. He is very hyper and constantly moving; you can't take your eyes off him for a minute. He plays like a wild child: he runs, jumps, and rolls around the apartment like he is outdoors. And don't let him go outside; it's worse. The outside air seems to give him super powers; he becomes Super Brat and gets so involved in his playtime that he refuses to listen to what anyone has to say. My mom is always asking me to help her watch him. It's not my job to help her with him. I have things to do that do not include a little boy. Besides I didn't ask to have a baby brother. I was perfectly content as an only child.

Also, Jay does not understand the meaning of personal space. The little fink clings to me like glue. I can't shake him; he is my shadow. When I move, he moves. I also have to watch cartoons with him every day after school. I am not interested in cartoons, but if I do not sit down with him he will be all over the apartment, and mom complains that she needs time to unwind after work. She acts as if my going to school is a piece of cake. I need time to wind down myself, but no one ever considers my needs or feelings.

Well, back to this family dinner. My parents were being so nice to each other it was scary. My dad asked my mom about her day. She didn't just tell him about today; I think she told him about every day. I guess she had to make up for lost time. Her face just lit up like a Christmas tree as she talked about her job. She went on and on, and my dad really appeared to be listening. I tell you, Diary, something is not right. She sells floor coverings for Christ's sake. How exciting can it be to sell tile and wood floors?

They continued to laugh and talk through most of the meal. Then, they turned their attention to Jay. Dad asked him about his favorite cartoon. I could tell him about his favorite cartoon, because I've watched it with Jay every day for the last two years. Jay told him about the many powers of Lord Zion. He even stood up and demonstrated some of the moves. He jumped, kicked and spun around, just like the cartoon. My parents laughed and clapped during his demonstration. My mom even told him to show her the jump kick again. I tell you Diary something is not right.

And then, it was my turn. My mom asked me about my friend, Tori. I looked up from my plate in surprise. Apparently, it was my time to share. So I told them that I had not spoken to Tori in months. They both looked surprised. That shows how little attention they give me. I went on to say, "Not since she stole my boyfriend." My dad coughed and repeated, "Boyfriend."

"Well, Levi could have been my boyfriend, if you guys would just treat me like a teenager instead of a child." I turned to my mom and said, "Remember when I asked you about going to the movies a couple of months ago, and you refused to let me go because the movie was rated 'R'?"

Mom nodded yes.

"Well, Tori's mom let her go, and guess who she ran into at the theater?"

My dad replied, "Levi?" He smiled as if it was funny, but it wasn't funny to me.

My mom said, "Honey, you and Tori have been friends since you were in grade school. Are you sure about the facts?"

I told her yes, I was sure, because Cindy Mason's brother saw Tori and Levi sitting beside each other during the movie. "Tori denies it, but why would Cindy's brother lie?"

My mom and dad both looked at each other and smiled. I knew they were silently laughing at me. I became furious. Why were they making fun of me? As I stood up to leave the table, my dad grabbed my arm. He put his arms around me and apologized. It was also a real hug not just a passing hug of convenience. He said he was sorry that Tori and I could not work out this problem. He also said it was time he started to realize that I was growing up and beginning to have grown up problems.

I sat back down at the table. I was anxious to see how the rest to this meal was going to unfold.

I was still unsure why my dad was home this early in the day. My dad is a supervisor for a large insurance company. He works in a large office building downtown. I don't remember what floor his office is on, but it's really high up. From his office window, I could see for miles across the city. I could tell he was an important person in his company, because the few times I had visited him at work I noticed that everyone in his office made it a point to say hello to him. Besides, as much as my dad works, he must be the most important person in the company. He works all the time and is rarely home. Most of the time he is either at the office or on a business trip out of town. When he is at home, he is working on his computer to complete the work he was unable to complete at the office. So even when he was home, he was not at home. For that reason, this sit-down family dinner caused me great concern.

I decided to ask my dad about his day. He smiled and said, "I'm glad you asked. I was laid off today."

He and my mom both continued to smile at each other. I was concerned. I knew that no job meant no income, and no income meant bills not being paid, and bills not being paid meant big trouble. I told you, Diary, something was not right.

He explained that his company was downsizing and that several positions had been eliminated. I was stunned. I knew something was wrong, but I never imagined this. My head quickly turned back and forth several times, looking at my mom and then my dad at opposite ends of the table. Several thoughts were racing through my head: I was wondering if we were going to have to move. I hoped my friends wouldn't find out that we are going to be poor. And most of all, I did not want to change schools and leave all my friends.

My dad told me to relax because everything was fine.

My response was to say, "What do you mean everything is fine, and why are the two of you so calm about this?"

My dad placed his hand on top of mine and asked, "Do you know how much I love you?"

I didn't say anything because I thought it might be a trick question. I just stared at him, because I didn't know where he was going with this. He said he had known he was in jeopardy of losing his job for months, and that he was only one of over two hundred people who were laid off within the last couple of months from his former company. He said he was upset in the beginning, especially when he thought about how he had dedicated the last twelve years of his life to his company. He thought about all the family activities he had missed because he was always working.

He was right. He never attended any of my dance recitals, school plays or my attempts at playing softball. He has never seen Jay play soccer with his youth league team. He really missed a treat.

He said that through his anger of being laid off, he realized that he had devoted most of his time in the wrong place. He looked at my mom and said, "Sometimes God is subtle when sending his messages; sometimes the messages need to be more obvious and hit you where it hurts most. My job had become my main focus. Today, God gave me a wakeup call. He has given me a second chance to get it right. My family is the most important thing in my life, second only to God

Almighty." He reassured me that financially we were fine, and there was no need for me to worry.

Well, Diary, can you believe that? I must tell you I was SHOCKED. My parents are still lame, but I must admit: today I see them in a new light.

Sunday Service

"Thank you, Lord, for blessing me with another day. As I enter into your house of worship, I give you all the honor and glory." Sundays are special to me because I have the opportunity to attend church service with my church family and hear the words of praise. I have been a member of this church for almost twenty years. I have seen many members come and go. Pastor Martin is the third pastor to become the leader of our flock during my tenure.

Regardless of the changes, Sunday church service is still my place of salvation. I always sit in the same seat some members have declared it my official permanent seat. It is near the back, on the right-hand side. I have the best seat in the house. I have a great view of the entire sanctuary. I can see almost everyone in attendance. I take pride in always being early for church services; I don't want to miss a minute of God's Word.

Look at Sister Mary Thomas. Here she comes again, down the church aisle, wearing her short dress. Just like every Sunday, she makes a grand entrance. Today, she has on a red skirt that is several inches above the knee with a split in the back that leaves nothing to the imagination. Plus, it's two sizes too small; she can barely walk. The tight white blouse she has on shows off her heavenly gifts and she *loves* to show off her heavenly gifts.

It takes her several minutes to sashay down the aisle as she continuously paused to speak to church members. She makes it a point to speak to certain male figures in the church. After her tour around the church, she finally sits on the front pew for everyone to see.

The Hardens are sitting three rows in front of me. They are sitting so close together it looks like they are on a date. He has his arm around her shoulder, and she is slightly leaning in towards him. I don't know why they are putting on this show, as if they are so in love. Just last Sunday the two of them refused to sit together during the church service. I don't know the exact nature of their dispute, but she came in first and sat near the front. He came in several minutes later and sat in the back even though there was room for him to sit next to his wife. After the service, he quickly exited the church doors without speaking a word to her. She stayed around for a short time to mingle, but whenever she was asked about her husband, she would not give a clear answer. To see the two of them now acting all lovey dovey in the House of the Lord is just wrong.

Oh my goodness! Ms. Minnie's hat caught my attention out of the corner of my eye. What in the world was she thinking? It looks like a ten-gallon hat that a cowboy from Texas would wear. Not only is it big, but it's light-blue with feathers. The feathers are blue, white, yellow, purple and so many other colors. It looks like her hat is about to take flight, or perhaps a flock of birds mistook her hat for their nest. I know the people sitting behind her must be furious; there is no way they can see the pulpit with that monstrosity sitting on her head.

The choir starts to sing, signifying the beginning of the service. I love to listen to the choir for the most part, although sometimes they sing songs I think are not appropriate for our church. I am from the old school and some of today's music is more about loud music and dancing than praising God. Through the harmony of the choir, I hear the voice of Sister Turly. Sister Turly is the loudest person in the choir. That would not be a problem if she could sing. I have always wondered what the requirements were to get into our church choir. I know it's not talent, because if it were Sister Turly would not be allowed to set one foot in the choir stand. The other choir members know she is their weakest link. They usually make sure she is never near any of the microphones, and she never has any major vocal parts during their performances. But today, Sister Turly means to be heard. I am embarrassed for her. She sounds like a seal with a sour throat. The agony could not end soon enough.

Brother Hill stands up and thanks the choir for the song selection. Then he says a few words about the song and what it means to him. Brother Hill is a good man, but public speaking is not his strong point. He speaks with a lisp. Some words he will never speak correctly, no matter how hard he tries. I linger on his every word, noting in my head each mispronunciation. He asks everyone to bow their heads as he reads the scripture. I counted six words this time. He's getting better.

The moment I have been waiting for finally arrives. Pastor Martin takes his place in the pulpit. Now *he* is a great speaker. You can tell he is a well-educated man. I am always impressed with his choice of words, even though I don't know what most of them mean. But he has a way of breaking down the scriptures so everyone from the small children to the elder members can understand. For some reason, today he is trying something different. He is walking from one end of pulpit to the other as he speaks. He is continuously moving back and forth. I am getting dizzy watching him. It's like I'm watching a tennis match and the ball is moving back and forth, back and forth. Finally, he stops. I think he got tired. He even sounds a little winded.

And will someone please wake up Deacon Edwards? His eyes have been closed since the beginning of the service. He always sleeps during the church services, and everybody acts like they don't notice. He sits straight up with is head bowed down, as if he's praying. He is sleeping so hard that his heavy breathing must be distracting to the people around him. The rumor is he has a tendency to drink a little too much a little too often. His wife died a couple of years ago, and he has not been the same since. He was married to a wonderful woman, Sister Liz. They were the ideal couple. They were always together and they never missed a church service. He was so happy then, but to see him now, just a shell of the man he once was, is so sad. If his wife could see him now, she would be so disappointed.

The service starts at ten o'clock every Sunday morning. Why are people still entering the sanctuary at eleven o'clock? Do they not have clocks like the rest of us? Or is it that they think they are so special that it's okay for them to interrupt the pastor during his sermon? I wish he would do a sermon about the importance of being on time, but I'm sure the people who need to hear it most would be late or not show up at all.

The Devin twins are so cute. They are only a couple months old and today they have on matching pink outfits with pink bows in their hair. The girls are just as noisy as they are cute, and they are really cute. Apparently, their parents were under the impression that babies could attend church and pay attention like adults. Boy, they were in for a rude awakening. The girls have cried and screamed during most of the service. Mom and dad each have one of the girls and are trying everything they can to calm the babies. They have already tried giving them bottles and pacifiers. They tried rocking and bouncing, but nothing has worked. The babies refuse to cooperate—like most small babies. Luckily, their parents finally come to their senses, pack up the girls and leave the service early.

Now Sister Edna has to have her moment. It's been awhile since she had one of her Holy Ghost shoutin' dance performances. The Holy Spirit always seems to hit her right on cue after the pastor completes his sermon and the choir begins their final selection and invites everyone to come to the alter for prayer. Today she starts in her seat, humming and rocking back and forth, and then there she goes; yelling, "Glory, Glory, Glory!" Just like every other time. She stands and begins to stomp and dance around. The ushers rush to her rescue to try and calm her down, because a few years ago she fell during one of her performances and hurt her back. This time, she is easily contained, and the church service concludes without any injuries.

"Thank you God for allowing me to congregate with my church family and worship in your name. As I leave your House of Worship, I ask that you keep listening to my prayers and help me become a better Christian."

Ask and You Shall Receive

I learned at an early age that God answers prayers. So one day, as I sat at my kitchen table going through my stack of bills, I asked God to send me a husband who could financially support me and my daughter. Once a month, I went through the routine of attempting to pay my bills. I was so tried of shuffling my limited funds and deciding which bills to pay, because there was no way I could pay them all at once.

The bill collectors had me afraid to answer my phone. They were often rude and talked to me like I was a criminal. I tried to explain my situation, but they didn't care; they just wanted their money, and they didn't care how I got it. I can't blame them for being persistent, but they sure made my life miserable. I was so tried of struggling. I needed help! My mother always said that God answers prayers, so I closed my eyes, bowed my head, clutched my hands together under my chin and began to pray. I asked God for what I wanted. I asked for a husband to take me away from all my financial troubles.

A few days after my prayer, Haden Philmore walked into the office of Pacific Pharmaceutical, the company where I worked as a receptionist. He was the total package. He was tall, dark and handsome. He wore a navy-blue suit with a white shirt and a red tie. The tie was the perfect choice; it screamed confidence and success. As he walked towards my desk, we made eye contact. I smiled as he approached and he returned the smile.

He stopped a respectable distance from my desk and asked me, "How are you doing today?"

My smile turned into a huge grin because I was not use to clients being nice or even acknowledging my presence. Usually they made demands or walked past my desk as if it was a bother to be polite. But he was different. I continued to grin while trying to remain professional. "I'm doing well," I said, "Thank you for asking."

He extended his hand to me for a handshake and introduced himself. "My name is Haden Philmore, and I have an appointment with Mr. Howard."

I buzzed Mr. Howard's office. Mr. Howard, one of the company's vice presidents, instructed me to send him in. I was surprised because Mr. Howard usually made clients wait. He said it was a business tactic and that making a client wait was his way of controlling a meeting from beginning to end. But this time, he did not hesitate.

I stood up from my desk and asked Mr. Philmore to follow me to Mr. Howard's office.

He smiled and said, "You lead, and I'll follow."

Not long after he went into the office, two other company representatives also went into the office. This had to be an important meeting. It lasted about three hours. Finally, the office door opened and all four men walked out, laughing and patting each other on the back. Mr. Howard told me to cancel the rest of their meetings for the day because they were taking Mr. Philmore to lunch, and they would be gone for the rest of the day. This deal *must* be big, I thought, because the last time they took a client to lunch was when our company received a huge new contract. We all received bonuses that year. I wasn't sure what was going on, but their absence from the office was a welcome change.

For the next couple of days, the office was buzzing about the possibility of a big new contract for our company. Mr. Howard called a staff meeting to explain some of the details of the new deal and to clear up some of the rumors that were running rampant. He explained that our company was in discussions with the Adderson Group, a well-known medical research laboratory. This was big. This deal would put our little company on the map, although he stressed that there were still many details to be worked out before the deal was final. He also stated that representatives from the Adderson Group would be visiting our office and the manufacturing plant, because they wanted to see if our company was capable of carrying out their wishes. He stressed the importance of everyone working together to show the Adderson Group that our company ran like a well-oiled machine.

The possibility of our company expanding was a great opportunity, but I was more excited to learn that Mr. Philmore might be returning to our office. However, one week passed, and no one from the Adderson Group showed up. I began to wonder if I would ever see him again.

The next week, four representatives—two men and two women—from the Adderson Group showed up with all their gear, including laptops and other equipment that would be used to evaluate our company. Haden Philmore was not a part of the group. I was disappointed. I had been looking forward to seeing him. I tried to convince myself that maybe it was for the best, because for all I knew he didn't even know I existed.

Mr. Howard instructed me to escort the four-member team into the conference room. My job was to help make them as comfortable as possible. The team did not need much help with their equipment. I pointed out a few electrical outlets and gave a brief demonstration of our projector remote. My main duty was to keep the room fully stocked with food and beverages. Earlier that morning, I stocked the conference room with juice, coffee and pastries.

As I was getting a muffin for one of the ladies, in walks Haden Philmore. He greeted Mr. Howard with a handshake, and when he spoke to the four team members he called them all by their first names, but they referred to him as 'Mr. Philmore.' When I saw him, I quickly turned my back to him and pretended to clean up the breakfast area, because I didn't know what to do with myself.

He walked over to the coffee pot and poured himself a cup of coffee. He stood beside me. I could see him out of the corner of my eye, but I didn't want to make eye contact. My heart was pounding extremely hard and fast.

He looked at me and said, "Hello."

I looked at him and said, "Hello" in a calm soft voice, but in my head I was screaming, "HELLO!"

He said, "We met the last time I was here, but I didn't catch your name."

I told him my name was Ellen. He said, "Nice to see you again, Ellen," before turning to walk back to Mr. Howard.

I left the room because their meeting was about to start. As I went back to my desk, I thought, today is going to be a good day.

Later, my thoughts took me to wondering who Haden Philmore was, and what was he about? I didn't want to be obvious about my attraction for him, so I decided to play it cool.

When the meeting was over, the team members walked down the hall to explore the set-up of the company. Mr. Howard walked with Mr. Philmore into the lobby area. I tried to look busy again, and once again, before he walked out the door to leave, he made it a point to speak to me. "Goodbye Ellen," he said with a smile and a nod.

Mr. Howard looked at me with a huge grin and said, "I think he likes you."

I was thinking the same thing, but the situation called for modesty, so I just smiled a little and went back to work.

I stepped away from my desk for a few minutes to get some supplies, and when I returned there was a telephone message from Haden Philmore. Initially, I thought the message was for Mr. Howard, but he was calling to speak to me. He wanted to take me to dinner. He left his cell phone number for me to call with my answer.

I called him back as soon as I heard the message. There's a time to play hard-to-get, and there's a time to count your blessings. This tall, handsome, professional, successful man was interested in little ole me; I called that a blessing.

I told him I would love to have dinner with him. He suggested Friday night and I agreed because that would give me time to find a baby sitter. He asked about picking me up for our date, but I told him that I would meet him at the location. He asked if I knew Jasper's Place. I was familiar with the restaurant. It was an upscale steak house. I had never had the pleasure of dining there, but I heard the food was delicious, and the prices were outrageous. I agreed and we sat the time for seven o'clock.

He ended the call by saying he was looking forward to our date.

"Me too," I said. "Good-bye."

I had to tell someone. I called my friend Trellis, who also worked at the office. She was the receptionist for the west wing of the company. When I told her I had a date, she screamed with joy. It had been a long time since I had been on date. She knew I was looking for a husband, but she also knew I would not go out with just anyone.

I told her who he was, and she seemed genuinely impressed. We talked about what I should wear. She told me not to wear red because it was too suggestive, and she also warned against yellow because it portrayed me as boring and dull. I listened to her, but Trellis was in a dating rut herself, so I knew that while her advice was well intended it was also without merit. I asked her to babysit my daughter, Kalli, while I was on my date. She agreed because that would allow her to be there while I was getting dressed, which I didn't mind because I needed her support. I told Trellis not to tell anyone. I didn't want gossip and rumors to ruin my date before I had a chance to go on my date. We both agreed that Haden would be a great catch, and I had to bring my 'A' game.

Date Night. I wore a green dress with short sleeves and carried a matching green scarf on my arm. I carried the scarf just in case the night air became chilly or if the restaurant was cooler than I anticipated. As I drove to the restaurant, I contemplated turning around and going home, but I stayed the course and arrived at Jasper's Place on time. Valet parking was not a usual concept for me. It felt good not to worry about parking; I just handed over my keys.

When I walked inside, I saw Haden sitting at a table in the middle of the room. I gave a small wave to get his attention. He waved back, acknowledging my arrival. I was nervous; I hoped he didn't notice. He stood up and walked over to meet me. He thanked me for coming. In turn, I thanked him for inviting me. He escorted me to our table.

The evening started right. Haden pulled out my chair for me to sit down. He talked about how beautiful I looked, and I returned the compliment. He looked really nice. He wasn't wearing a business suit. He wore a nice sport jacket and slacks. He was casual yet classy. The waiter brought a bottle of wine to the table and poured us both a glass of red wine, and left the bottle at the table. I was impressed; it was obvious he put this into motion before my arrival.

Next the waiter brought menus to the table, but Haden didn't need to look at the menu. He ordered a steak with potatoes and mixed vegetables. I, on the other hand, was not familiar with the menu, so I read over the items a couple of times. I decided on baked fish. He complimented me on my choice.

Our conversation started when Haden asked me to tell him all about myself. The first thing I did was tell him about my six-year-old daughter. I wanted to see his reaction. Some men have trouble with women who have children. Surprisingly, he handled it well. He asked me if I had any pictures. Of course, I did. He laughed and smiled as we went through my small album of pictures and he said he hoped to meet her some day. Wow! I was pleasantly surprised. I wanted to know more about this man.

I learned he was twenty-eight, which was five years older than me. He was born on July 4th, had never married and had no children. No children that was a big plus. He was well educated with a MBA from Florida University, and he was not just an employee at the Adderson Group; he was one of the three owners.

We talked for hours. The restaurant closed at ten o'clock but it was after eleven and we were still there talking. No one told us to leave, but the restaurant staff began to clean up around us. I told him it was late and that I had to go home.

We stood in front of the restaurant while the valet retrieved my car. He asked for my phone number. I gave him my cell number with the condition that he had to call me. He agreed with a smile.

When my car arrived, he gave me a hug and kissed me on the cheek. The date was over, or so I thought. My phone rang as I drove out of the restaurant's parking lot. It was him. He said he just wanted to test the number. My apartment building was only about twenty minutes away from the restaurant and we were still talking when I reached the parking lot of my building. I stayed in my car, and we continued to talk. I hated to end our conversation, but it was late and I had to go inside and check on Kalli.

After our first date, our relationship developed very quickly. Our relationship was like a roller coaster ride. It was fun, exciting, and scary; but no matter how scary the ride, you keep getting back on because the good far out-weighs the bad. We were inseparable. We were together every spare moment we had. I introduced him to my daughter after only three weeks into the relationship. I usually waited several months before involving my daughter, but this time was different. I could feel it in my heart.

Soon afterwards, he met my mom and dad. My mom liked him from the start. She thought he was charming, and his financial stability was an added bonus. On the other hand, my dad was skeptical. He thought our relationship was moving too fast. But according to my dad, no one was good enough for his little girl. He was nice to Haden but it wasn't genuine. Nevertheless, my father's doubts didn't slow down our ride.

During our second month of dating, Haden paid for Kalli and me to fly first class from California to Florida to meet his mother and brother. His mother's home was beautiful and huge. I had seen homes like this on television, but to see one in person was amazing. There were four live-in servants. Kalli and I were in awe of such luxury, but Haden took it all in stride.

We met his mom first. She was a petite lady with a raspy voice. She greeted all of us with hugs; Haden first, then me, and then Kalli. She complimented Kalli on her beautiful golden hair and also gave her a gift. It was a pink video-game player with a couple of games. Kalli was surprised and pleased, and I was impressed that she had taken the time to do something for my daughter even before they met. His mother was so nice. She gave me a tour of her home and showed me baby pictures of Haden and his brother, Jack.

Jack arrived at the house a couple of hours after our arrival. He was also polite, but he was very talkative. Jack alluded to the possibility that Haden had an extensive history with women. This revelation was not shocking, although coming from his brother, it was in poor taste.

We were in Florida for four glorious days. Kalli and I were treated like royalty. Money was no object. We dined at expensive restaurants and shopped at exclusive boutiques. Sightseeing from the window of a limousine was the highlight of the trip for Kalli.

Before we left, Haden's mom thanked us for coming and hugged all three of us as we were walking out the door. When she hugged me, she whispered in my ear, "I look forward to seeing you again." All I could do was smile. She liked me; that was *my* highlight of the entire trip.

We returned home and continued our journey. Three months into our relationship, I mentioned to Haden that I was considering getting a second job. He wouldn't hear of it. He insisted that I allow him to help me financially. He did more than help; he took care of all my bills and gave me additional money for incidentals. I continued working at Pacific Pharmaceutical, but my money troubles were distant memories. Life was good. God had answered part of my prayer. I wasn't married, but I could answer my phone again.

After five months of dating, Haden sold his stock in the Adderson Group. He also accepted a position with a research firm in Florida. I didn't know about any of this until everything was final. The ultimate surprise was that he included me and Kalli in his plans. He asked me to marry him and go to Florida with him.

I didn't hesitate. I said, "Yes!!!"

We were married on June 3rd in a small ceremony on a beach in Florida. After the ceremony, there was another revelation. He had bought us a house on the beach. I was living a fairytale. My prayers had been answered; I was married and financially secure.

I should have been the happiest person in the world, but I wasn't. Soon after we moved to Florida, things started to change. Haden traveled a lot with his new job. Most of the time, Kalli and I were home alone. It would not have been so bad if we were still in California, but we were in Florida. I didn't know anyone there but his mother and brother. I had hoped to develop a relationship with the two of them, but that never came to pass. Haden didn't want me to visit with them or with anyone else. He wanted me at home all the time, even when he wasn't there. When he was away, he would call to check up on me. If I wasn't at home, he wanted details of what I did, who I saw and who I spoke with. Once I went to a meeting at Kalli's school, but he thought I was gone too long so he took my car keys for a week. When I needed to go somewhere, he took me.

I no longer had money problems, but Haden controlled what I spent. Shopping was a family outing. He never let me buy anything without his approval. I wasn't working outside the home; therefore, I had no income in his eyes. It was his money, and he controlled every dime.

After two years of marriage, I was not happy. I tried to talk to Haden about our marriage, but he insisted that everything was fine and that I was over-reacting. I didn't know what to do. Was God punishing me for something? Then I remembered the prayer, I made a couple of years earlier. I asked God to send me a husband who would take care of Kalli and me financially. God had given me exactly what I asked for.

Be careful what you pray for; you just might get it.

Real Men Don't Cry??

My best friend was killed last year in a car accident. He was killed instantly when his car ran off the road and hit a tree. According to the accident report, he lost control of his car. The accident occurred in broad daylight, it wasn't raining, he wasn't sick, he wasn't drinking, and he was not speeding. Mark had driven that road numerous of times. Why was that time any different? It's difficult to believe he just lost control of his vehicle.

It was his wife, Beth, who called to tell me about his death. She wasn't crying, but I could tell something was wrong. She told me Mark had been in an accident. I asked if he was okay. She said no. She didn't say anything else.

She didn't have to say it; I knew. I told her I was on my way.

Mark and Beth had three children; two sons and a daughter. Troy was sixteen, Marcus was ten and Alisa was nine. I needed to be with his family. Mark was not my brother by blood, but he was my brother nonetheless.

I called my wife to let her know what happened. She was asking for details, but I didn't know any details. All I knew was that my friend was dead and my heart was hurting. She agreed to meet me at their family home.

While I was driving to his house, there was a large lump in my throat and my eyes were filled with tears. I quickly wiped away my tears because I had to be strong for the family. The family needed the presence of a strong man, and I did not want them to see me weak and crying.

When I arrived, I saw there were several cars parked at his house, some in the driveway and others on the side of the street. I had to park three houses away. As I walked to the house, a feeling of fear came over me. I was literally afraid. I didn't know what to expect in the house.

I stopped to get myself together. I closed my eyes and took several deep breaths. Again, I told myself I had to be strong for the family. Once I was composed, I proceeded to the house. There were several people standing outside the house in the yard. I was stopped several times. It seemed as if everyone wanted to give me a hug or shake my hand. I was cordial, but I wanted everyone to leave me alone so I could go into the house and see the family.

When I walked in the door the first person I saw was Mama Faye, Mark's mom. She was sitting on the couch surrounded by several people. When she saw me, she rose to her feet, walked over and gave me hug. She asked me what took me so long too get there. I told her I came as soon as I heard. She put her head to my chest and started to cry. I held her tight. I wanted her to know that I loved her and that I was there for her as long as she needed me. Mark didn't have any biological brothers, and his dad died several years ago.

He had one sister, Rae, but she lived in another state. After a few minutes, Mama Faye wiped her eyes and told me Rae was on her way.

I asked her to tell me what happened. She took my hand and walked me into the dining room. We sat at the dining room table. At the time, all she knew was that he hit a tree and died from a severe head injury. Her voice trembled as she spoke. She said he had his seatbelt on, like he was supposed to, but this still happened. Tears began to flow down her cheeks again.

I pulled my chair closer and put my arm around her. I told her that everything was going to be okay, but in my heart I wasn't sure if everything was going to be okay. I knew that I would never be the same. Several people walked into the dinning room to offer their condolences. Mama Faye soon decided that she needed a break, so she went into the guest bedroom to take a nap. I told her I would check on her in a few minutes.

Beth was standing behind me as I closed the guest bedroom door. Her eyes were a dark shade of red and her entire face was puffy. We hugged each other, and she said, "Good to see you." I asked her how she was holding up. She said she was not good; there was so much to be done, and she didn't know where to start. She said Mark had always handled all their financial business, and she never paid attention. I remembered that Mark had once told me Beth hated paying bills, so he had taken on the task so she would not be stressed. That was part of his way of taking care of his family.

I told her not to worry; I would help her with the funeral arrangements and we would go through all their financial documents together. I saw a look of relief in her eyes. She said thanks and gave me another hug before walking away. I knew she had to make the rounds to her other guests.

At that point, I started to look for the kids. I found Marcus and Alisa in Marcus's room. Marcus as playing a video game on the television, and Alisa was playing a game on the computer. When I entered the room, Alisa ran to me and gave me hug, just like she always did. I held her a little longer this time and kissed her on top of her head.

I had to ask Marcus for a hug. He made me wait while he paused his game, but that was cool. I didn't pressure him. I sat on the bed, and Alisa sat beside me.

She said, "I can't believe he's gone."

I agreed with her and said, "I know."

Marcus turned around in his chair to face us on the bed. He said, "You guys talk about him being gone as if he is on a trip. He's not on a trip; he's dead; D-E-A-D dead." He turned his chair back around and start to play his video game again.

I put my hand on his should and said, "I'm going to miss him too."

His game controller fell out of his hand. He put his hands over his face and began to cry. I dropped to one knee to give him a hug. Alisa joined in the hug; she was also in tears. I stayed with them for a long time. I told them funny stories about their dad. They needed me, and I was glad to be there for them.

Troy walked into the room to tell me that my wife had arrived. I tried to stop him, but he made a quick exit. I didn't chase him. He and I would talk when the time was right.

My wife, Shannon, was sitting at the kitchen table with Beth. They were not best friends, but they were friendly with each other. Besides, our families spent a lot of time together, and I hoped that would continue. I kissed Shannon on the cheek. She asked me how I was doing, and I told her I was doing okay.

Beth complimented me on my willingness to help her get her affairs in order; Shannon also offered her assistance. Beth smiled and said she needed all the help she could get. She then asked me if I had had a chance to speak with the kids. I told her I had spoken with Marcus and Alisa, but not with Troy.

With tears in her eyes, she said, "Please speak with him before you leave. He's having a hard time." She thought he was trying to stay strong for the family, but she didn't want him to carry that burden. She had tried to talk with him earlier, but at the time he was unwilling to listen. I told her I would not leave before speaking with him.

When I went in search of Troy, I didn't have to look far. He was in the living room receiving advice from well-meaning family members and friends. His uncle Willis, Beth's brother, told him he was the man of the house now and that he had to look out for the family. Another person told him he was just like his father. The most absurd advice was that he had to put away childish things, because he had to be a father figure for his sister and brother. I had heard enough. It angered me that these adults were trying to take away his childhood. Troy was still a boy, and he was not going to become a man overnight. I interrupted and invited Troy to play a game of basketball. He quickly agreed, and as we left the room he thanked me for rescuing him.

On the way to the makeshift basketball court in the backyard, Troy picked up his basketball and started to dribble. He passed the ball to me and asked if I wanted to play one on one. I accepted his challenge, although I knew I didn't stand a chance. He was a first string point guard for his high-school basketball team. I, on the other hand, was twenty pounds over-weight, and basketball was not my sport of choice. Nevertheless, we played for about an hour. During the game, we didn't talk about his dad. He gave me pointers on how to improve my game. I tried his suggestions, but I still lost.

After my embarrassing loss, we sat on a bench near the court. I needed to catch my breath, although Troy had barely broken a sweat. While looking at his basketball twirling in his hands, he thanked me for not telling him how he's supposed to feel. He said everybody wanted to talk to him and give him advice, but he just wanted to be left alone. I told him I knew the feeling.

He stopped twirling the ball and placed it on the ground. He looked at me and asked if I cried when I found out. I told him no. I lied. I didn't want him to see me as weak. He said me he hadn't cried either. I told him it was okay for him to cry, because he was still a kid. I didn't want him to think he had to instantly grow up and become a man. He said he wasn't trying to be a grownup; crying would mean that he accepted his dad's death, and he wasn't ready to do that. I told him that everyone had their own way of dealing with grief, but he didn't have to go through it alone. He nodded his head; he knew he had people who loved him.

I patted him on the back and suggested we go back inside. He didn't move. He told me to go ahead; he wanted to stay a little longer.

I could tell he was getting emotional and wanted to be alone.

While I was walking back towards the house, I looked back to check on him. I saw him lowering his head and crying. At that moment, the pain in my heart was unbearable. I fell to my knees, and the rest of my body went limp. I wasn't just crying; I was sobbing.

Troy came up behind me and put his arms around me. We were both crying, but he was more in control than I was. I told him I was sorry for breaking down. He said there was no need to apologize. He helped me to stand on my feet. He smiled and said, "I see real men do cry." He made me laugh. I should have been comforting him, but he was comforting me instead.

It has been a little over a year since Mark's death. Everyday gets a little better. I remained close with Beth and all three children. My eyes still get misty when I think about the freak accident that took away my best friend (my brother). I am no longer ashamed of my tears. It took a boy to teach me what it means to be a man.

Blessed

"London bridges, falling down, falling down, falling down; London bridges falling down, my fair lady," I watched and listened to the joyful sounds of my two girls playing outside on a warm spring afternoon. Trinity and Talya are eleven months apart, although most people think they are twins. Trinity is the oldest, but it's Talya who has taken on the role of "big sister." They are very different, but inseparable.

Talya is confident and very outgoing. We refer to her as the "boss." Whenever she is playing with her sister or other children in the neighborhood, she decides what games they are going to play. Her interpretations of the rules are usually swayed to benefit her likes and dislikes. She can be very persuasive, and the other children rarely challenge her ideas.

Trinity is the opposite. She is shy and very reserved. She doesn't make a move without Talya's input. Sometimes, she looks to Talya to help her complete her sentences. The girls truly complement each other.

Talya was born with spinal bifida. In simple terms, she was born with a hole in her spine. She has gone through several surgeries and illnesses throughout her short life. She had two major surgeries by age three. The first was to repair her spine and possibly give her some movement of her lower body. Unfortunately, seven years later she is still unable to walk. The second surgery was to help with her bladder problems. That surgery was considered a success because she does have some control of her bladder. She still has accidents occasionally, but in the scheme of every thing she has gone through, we can live with a few accidents. She has also had several bouts with bladder and kidney infections.

However, during every health crisis or hospital stay, Talya has never lost her upbeat spirit. She is always trying to make everyone around her smile and feel better about the situation. Trinity's devotion to her sister is immeasurable. The girls always want to be together, regardless of the location or the circumstance.

Talya's health issues have been a continuous struggle for her and our entire family. My husband, Tony, is a truck driver. He took on additional routes to help pay the medical bills. He is rarely home, but we understand, although I hate that he is missing out on watching the girls grow up. I work part-time at my father's hardware store. My father is very accommodating when I need to be off to take care of the girls. He is not able to pay much, but every little bit helps.

About six months ago, Talya was hospitalized for three days. She had an infection that started in her bladder, but later spread into her bloodstream. This hospital stay was one of the worst. There were several tubes and medical machines attached to her little body. The machines were beeping to the rhythm of her heart. It was a comforting sound, because her heartbeat was strong, but the oxygen tube in her nose was disturbing because it seemed to cause her discomfort.

Trinity didn't seem to notice any of the equipment. She was just happy to be with her sister. She would tell Talya about her day at school; she didn't want her to miss a thing. If Talya was sleeping, Trinity would just hold her hand and watch cartoons on the television. When it was time for her to go home, she was always disgruntled.

To have both girls at home, happy and healthy, is the greatest gift God could have given me. I can watch them play for hours. Their laughter is music to my ears.

I heard Talya ask Trinity if she wanted to go inside and play with the dolls. Trinity agreed and pushed Talya in her wheelchair inside. Talya doesn't usually need or want help with her wheelchair, so I thought she was just letting Trinity be helpful. Talya stayed in the living room while Trinity went to their bedroom to get the dolls.

As Trinity left the room, Talya told me she wasn't feeling well. She said she was tried and felt sick to her stomach. I asked her how long she had felt sick, and she said, "Since last night."

I was upset that she had waited so long to tell me.

She said, "I promised Trinity we would play today. When I am sick, it makes her sad, and I didn't want her to be sad today. No matter how much pain I feel, I know Trinity feels ten times worse. She says a prayer for me every morning and every night. In the morning, she asks God to let me have a good day without any pain; and at night she asks God to let me make it through the night because she cannot live without me."

My anger quickly turned into admiration and compassion. I kissed her on the forehead. I always knew my girls were special, but I had no idea just how truly blessed I am.

Thanksgiving Dinner

Atlanta, Georgia is a twelve-hour drive from Cleveland, Ohio, but once again I travel this long journey alone going home for Thanksgiving. I left Cleveland early Tuesday morning. It was still dark out when I put my car on the road; I wanted to start my drive in minimal traffic. I phoned my mom to let her know I was on my way home. She sounded unusually lively, even though it was extremely early. She made me promise that I would not speed. I grudgingly agreed, but that was a difficult promise to keep.

Thanksgiving dinners have always been a special time for my family. Each year, I always looked forward to seeing my parents and my four siblings. My parents have been married for thirty-two years. My dad says it was love at first sight, but my mom says she had to mold him into her dream beau. Although they disagree on their beginning, there is no arguing that their relationship works and they have thirty-two years of experience to prove it.

I have one sister and three brothers. My brother, Larry Jr., is the oldest; Jeff is next; and then Edwin. I am the fourth child, and Cassie is the baby. When we were small children, Thanksgiving dinners were simple. But now, everyone has grown up and moved way. All my brothers are married and have children of their own. My sister is married, with no children. I am divorced with no children. We all have our own lives, but Thanksgiving is the time we all get together.

I remember the Thanksgiving dinners when we were young children. Grandpa was the life of the party. He always had a pocket full of quarters. He would ask all the kids questions, and if we got the answers right, he gave us quarters. He would ask simple questions like, "How do you spell your name?" "How old are you?" and, "Who is the best grandpa in the whole world?" For years, I thought grandpa was a walking bank. He seemed to have an endless supply of quarters. I treasured every quarter, but most of all I treasured the time I spent with him. He truly was the best grandpa in the whole world.

One of my most memorable Thanksgiving dinners was the time my brother invited two girls and they both showed up. The doorbell rang, and Larry quickly ran out of his bedroom to answer the door. Before he opened the door, he looked out the peep hole and then turned and gave everyone instructions. He told Cassie not to ask so many questions; he told Edwin and Jeff to mind their manners; and then he looked at me and said to be nice. My dad told him to hurry up and open the door before the girl changed her mind.

He opened the door, and in walked a girl we had never seen before. We were all surprised because we had been expecting, his girl-friend, Jasmine. I looked at Cassie; Jeff looked at Edwin; mom and dad were also surprised.

Mom was the first to speak. She told Larry to introduce his friend. Her name was Teresa. She was not as pretty as Jasmine, and she was also on the heavy side. Jasmine was tall and thin. I liked Jasmine. Therefore, I knew I was not going to like this Teresa.

As soon as she sat down on the couch next to Larry, Cassie began her interrogation of the poor girl. She asked every question she could think of. Larry told her to stop asking so many questions, but Cassie was relentless. Teresa was nice enough to answer every question; she even asked Cassie a few questions of her own.

Cassie seemed to be impressed, but I was going to be loyal to Jasmine.

Finally, mom called everyone into the kitchen because dinner was ready. Cassie made it a point to sit by Teresa. We were all seated and preparing to say the blessing when the doorbell rang again. This time my dad told Jeff to answer the door because he was closest.

Jeff went to the door and looked through the peephole. However, he did not open the door; instead he called for Larry.

When Larry went to the door, Jeff returned to the table with a strange look on his face. No one asked who was at the door. We all knew it had to be Jasmine. What an awkward situation for everyone. We just sat there at the table, not saying a word.

We couldn't hear the actual words of the heated discussion between Larry and Jasmine, but we could tell the conversation was not friendly. I could not believe that Teresa just sat there without saying a word.

I knew she had to be uncomfortable, but she never broke a sweat. She just smiled the entire time.

A few minutes later, Larry re-entered the dining room and sat down next to Teresa.

Dad asked, "Is everything okay?"

Larry's response was, "Everything is just as it should be." He kissed Teresa on the cheek and held her hand. At that moment, I changed my allegiance. I could tell that Larry really liked this girl; if he was willing to kiss her in front of all of us, she must be special. Teresa, my sister-in-law, has been a part of our lives ever since.

I also can't forget the Thanksgiving dinner dad announced he was retiring from the post office. After everyone had finished eating, my dad had called everyone into the family room. We'd had family meetings before, so this was nothing new. My dad was sitting in his chair. My mom was standing behind him with her hands on his shoulders. He placed his left hand on top of hers and told us about his retirement.

I never thought he would retire; he loved his job. The people he worked with were like members of our family. His coworkers were always invited to our home for every birthday and holiday celebrations. I was shocked, but happy for him. If anyone deserved to relax in his glory years, it was my dad.

He then went on to say that he and mom were going to do some traveling. He held up two tickets to Miami, Florida, where they planned to go for Christmas. That was the first time my parents had ever planned a trip without including any other family members.

They were like two school-age teenagers, whispering and giggling about the fun they were going to have without any children around. They even spoke of moving to Miami to enjoy the sunny weather.

Although I was happy for them, I was scared, because I could not imagine them living anywhere else and I wondered what would to happen to our home if they moved to Miami. Miami would add several additional miles to my travels.

They traveled to Miami that Christmas, but thank God the permanent move never came to pass. My parents are still in Atlanta, and I am headed home once again.

Last Thanksgiving, Cassie announced she was pregnant. The family was so excited. Cassie and I were the last of our siblings who did not have children. The pressure to have a baby in our family was overwhelming. Questions of our ability to bear children were always on the tip of everyone's tongue. I think the pressure was greater for Cassie because she and her husband, Alex, had been trying to conceive for years. I was the divorced sister; therefore, that was my excuse. Now, after her announcement, all eyes were going to be focusing on me.

Cassie was two months pregnant. Mama said she knew it because she had a dream about fish. I was not sure what fish had to do with having a baby, but we never questioned mama and her supernatural abilities. They didn't know the sex of the baby, but they had decided on names. They were going to name the child after Alex's brother, Sam, who was killed in Iraq. They were so happy, and we all treated them extra special.

Samantha Catherine was born on April 14th. We were not expecting her until June, so her premature delivery caused great concern. She was so tiny; she weighed only three pounds and six ounces. Her little body was so frail. The doctors did everything they could, but Samantha died three days later. Cassie was so amazing during that time. She had every right to be mad, angry and bitter, but somehow she chose to approach her loss with a positive outlook and trusting in God.

I knew Cassie and Alex had previously become 'saved.' I guess I did not really understand the meaning of being a Christian or being 'saved,' because I was having trouble dealing with Samantha's death. I needed Cassie to explain her new religious ideas to me. She spoke of her faith in God and how she knew that his will was just. I became angry with her, because how could she think that an innocent baby dying was just?

She could tell I was angry. She said, "Let me explain. I have good days and bad days. I grieve for the daughter I lost, because I would have loved to watch her grow up, and that will never happen. But I have no doubt that Samantha is in heaven surrounded by people who love her, and that gives me peace. As a Christian, I can't just pick and choose when I am going to have faith in God. My faith is not something I put on the shelf and pull out when times are good. Faith is most important when we encounter low points in our lives."

Cassie and I have spoken on the phone several times since that conversation, but this Thanksgiving dinner is going to be the first time I have seen her since Samantha's graveside service. I am so excited about seeing her, because she inspired me to start going to church. I can't wait to tell her I have joined a church. I have just begun to learn about the teachings of Jesus Christ so I won't say I am 'saved,' but I am working on it.

With several miles to go before I reach home, I take comfort in knowing God is my co-pilot and I have nothing to worry about. I will be home eating Thanksgiving dinner with my family before I can say "Happy Thanksgiving."

Best Friends Forever (BFF)

Leigh and I are best friends. We have been best friends since the sixth grade. Leigh moved into the house across the street from mine. The first day the Neal family moved in, my mom and I took them some homemade chocolate-chip cookies to welcome them to the neighborhood. I was so excited to learn that the new neighbors had a daughter the same age as me. We were both eleven and in the sixth grade. Leigh and I became friends instantly.

I found out very quickly that the Neal family was very religious. After only one week of meeting Leigh, she asked me to go to church with her and her parents. She explained that her entire family attended church every Sunday. My family was not your average church family. We only attended church on special occasions and holidays. We mainly went to church on Easter Sunday. I always looked forward to Easter because I always got a new dress and shoes to match. Mom and I always went alone. Dad was usually working or had other plans.

So when Leigh asked me to go to church, I was skeptical about going because it wasn't a holiday, a wedding or a baptism. It was just Sunday. But, I agreed to go, and I had a good time. To my surprise, the kids did not have to stay seated with the grownups. We were moved into another room away from the grownups.

The Youth Minister made learning about God fun. We did not have to sit in our seats for two hours and stay quiet. We were allowed to talk and ask questions. Wow! I never knew church could be so much fun.

Leigh started school during the middle of the year. She was so scared, but I knew my way around the sixth-grade and was not going to let anything happen to her. I introduced her to all my friends, and pretty soon my friends were her friends. We had one class together: music. I played the clarinet, and Leigh played the flute. We would make plans to practice after school, but all too often it turned into talking, listening to music, and playing outside. We rarely got in any practice time.

When we reached the eighth-grade, Leigh was the first to have a boyfriend in our little group. Some of the girls were jealous and started to say mean things about her. They talked about her clothes, her hair, and her choice for a boy friend. They even said she was doing things with this boy. That was so far from the truth. Leigh was a Christian, and she would never do anything against her faith. She only talked with him on the phone and at school. Her parents would not allow her to officially date. Teenage girls can be really mean.

High school seems like only yesterday. We went through so many changes during that time. My parents divorced when I was in the tenth grade, and my father moved out of the house. Leigh's mom got a job outside of the home after years of being a stay-at-home mom. I continued to play my clarinet, while Leigh decided that she was no longer interested in playing her flute. We went through several haircuts and hair colors, and we started to realize that boys were a dime a dozen. Leigh and I made new friends and started to run in different circles. I hung out with the band kids, so most of my activities were centered around my music. Leigh was not involved in that part of my life. She loved sports and was great at basketball and volleyball. She was part of the athletic group. She was a jock and proud of it. We both did our own thing.

The more things changed the more they stayed the same. Through all our changes, Leigh and I remained friends. I no longer went to church with Leigh every Sunday, but I made it a point to go at least once a month. We didn't talk every day like we used to, but when we talked we discussed everything from A to Z. I wanted to hear about everything going on in her life, and I was eager to share my adventures and escapades. We no longer had the same interests, but our bond was still strong.

With high school coming to an end, Leigh and I made a pact to make sure that no matter where we were, we would stay in contact and keep a relationship with Christ. We promised to contact each other on our birthdays, and Leigh made me promise to attend church at least once a month. We hooked our right pinky fingers together to seal our pact just like we had done when we were kids.

On graduation day, our parents gave us a party in my backyard. The party was fun while it lasted. We both cried and hugged each other. We realized that our lives would take us in different directions. No longer would I have satisfaction of knowing that Leigh, my best friend, was across the street.

After the family party, she and I went our separate ways. She left with her friends, and I went with mine.

She didn't forget. When my birthday came that year, I wondered if she would remember our pact. She did; she called and asked if I wanted to go to dinner to celebrate my birthday. A couple of months later, I returned the favor on her birthday. Leigh continued to go to church every Sunday, and I kept my promise to go at least once a month.

Over the years, our lives continued to go down different paths. My mom remarried and moved out of our family home. Leigh's parents are still married and continue to live in the old neighborhood. I am married with two children, while Leigh is single with no children. Through all our changes and differences, Leigh and I have never missed a birthday, and I kept my promise to attend church, although my promise to her turned out to be more than I ever imagined.

My monthly church attendance turned into weekly attendance. My weekly attendance turned into daily prayer. My daily prayer turned into a way of life. I can never thank Leigh enough for introducing me to my Lord and Savior. Now days, we rarely see each other, but our bond is strong. When we made that promise so many years ago, I had no idea the impact it would have on my life. Leigh is my BFF 'Best Friend Forever.'

Who Are These People?

I was twelve when my mother passed away. I still recall her funeral like it was yesterday. The church was filled with so many people. I knew a few of them, but most of them were strangers. I had never seen that many people gathered together in one room before in my life. When we walked into the church, everyone was standing. As I walked down the aisle holding hands with my grandmother, I observed several sad faces in the crowd. Some people were weeping quietly while others were crying loudly. I gazed around the church at all the people and asked myself, "Who are these people?"

At the end of the aisle, I saw my mama. She looked as if she was just sleeping. I was old enough to know that she was dead, but seeing her was bittersweet. She was wearing her floral dress, which she had bought the last time we went shopping. Her casket was light blue, her favorite color and surrounded by lots of beautiful flowers. I stood in front of her casket for several minutes. My grandmother didn't rush me to sit down. She told me to take my time.

Eventually, I sat down beside my grandmother on the front pew. As I sat there on the hard wooden pew, an elderly woman I did not know began to fan me. I was grateful for the fanning, because the temperature in the church had risen several degrees. I continued to gaze around the church at all the people. Again, I asked myself, "Who are these people?"

The preacher started the funeral service by saying "We are gathered here today to celebrate the home-going of Sister Lorraine Burton." The word "celebrate" pulsated in my head. I could not believe he said "celebrate." He started to quote Bible verses and speak in rhymes. It seemed as if the more he spoke, the louder he got. He talked about my mama as if he knew her. He didn't know her. We only attended church on special occasions with my grandmother. The service seemed to go on forever. I became irritated at the tone of the lengthy service. The preacher ended his performance by saying, "She is in a better place." The audience said, "Amen." Again, I asked myself, "Who are these people?"

I am all grown up now, and I can't thank my grandmother enough for taking on the challenge of raising me after my mom's death. She was there for my lows and my highs. She was there when Jamal Wilkens stood me up for what was supposed to be my first official date. That day, she and I ate ice cream and talked for hours about the many flaws of men and boys. She was there when it was announced that I was the first African American Valedictorian for my high school. She was so proud of me. She didn't have to say it with words I could see it in her eyes, behind the tears.

But, life has once again thrown me for a loop. My grandmother was recently diagnosed with Alzheimer's. It's so hard for me to believe this is happening. How could God do this to me twice? I lost mom-number-one to cancer, and now I am losing mom-number-two to forgetfulness. Could God be so cruel? My grandmother is the healthiest person I know. She never gets sick. I don't think she has ever had a cold. She contributes her good health to her faith in God.

She is known as Sister Dottie in her church, which she has always attended faithfully. Before her illness, if the church doors were open, my grandmother was there. She was there every Sunday for the eight o'clock service and always stayed for Sunday school. Wednesday night service was not complete if Grandmother was not heard from the Amen Corner. In the beginning of our lives together, I regularly attended church with her, but as I got older I went less and less. She would always encourage me to go with her, but she never forced me. She always said, "God wants willing souls—not souls held hostage."

The rare times I attended her church, the members acted like they were so pleased to see me. But I did not feel comfortable in church because they did not know me, just like they did not know my mother years earlier. I have mixed feelings about God, church and church folk. I would never voice these feelings to my grandmother because that would break her heart. I know there is a God, because he gave me two wonderful mothers, but is he also responsible for the suffering of both amazing women?

My grandmother is also well known for her dedication to our community. She believed that our neighborhood was an extension of our home. Before her illness, she was always involved in one community project after another. She was the driving force behind our first neighborhood-watch after an elderly woman who lived on our block was attacked in her home. Although my grandmother was older than the victim, she was the first to stand up and insist that something be done to make our neighborhood safe. She would patrol the streets of our neighborhood as if she was a trained police officer.

She was devoted to giving back to the community. She volunteered at the local community food bank, delivered meals and visited people who were unable to leave their homes. She was also a vocal recruiter of voter registration. She was passionate about all her causes, but voter registration held a special place in her heart. She had grown up during the Civil Rights Movement and spoke often of her experiences during that time of injustice and inequality. She stressed that the right to vote was earned through blood, sweat and tears and therefore it was everyone's responsibility to carry on the legacy.

With all her volunteer duties, she still found time to go to her real job. Of course, she would tell you that she works for the Lord, but her job at the local paper mill is what paid the bills. I always told her that she needed to slow down, but she would not hear of it.

Her diagnosis of Alzheimer's really caught me off guard. I never saw any signs until she was having major problems with her memory. I am a junior at Jefferson University, but I live at home. I chose Jefferson University because it was local, and I wanted to be near my grandmother. She was changing right under my nose, but I was so involved in my own life that I was not there for her when she needed me most.

After she was diagnosed, I decided to take a break from school to devote my time to taking care of her. Sister Gladys, who is a member of the Amen Corner at Grandmother's church, caught wind of my plans to postpone my education. She was not happy with my decision. She told me, "Sister Dottie has worked hard to see you graduate from college." I told her that I would go back someday, but first I needed to take care of my grandmother. However, Sister Gladys was adamant about the fact that Grandmother would not approve of my plan. She offered her services to help take care of my grandmother, and I agreed to stay in school. I knew she was right; Grandmother would not have been happy if I postponed my education.

Under Sister Gladys' guidance, the ladies of the Amen Corner stayed with Grandmother during the day. Every morning, one or two elderly ladies from her church arrived at our home to help start our day. Breakfast was always the first order of business. Grandmother likes toast and scramble eggs; the ladies never disappoint her. Lunch and dinner were also provided, and they made sure to provide enough for me as well. They also keep her company during the day. Now days, Grandmother is not much of a talker, but it doesn't seem to matter to the ladies. They talk to her continuously, and sometimes she recognizes their faces, and they have moments of genuine discussions.

The ladies also made sure that she attended church services every Sunday. They organized a system for transporting her there and back. They knew how much she loved to be in the House of the Lord. Most of the time, I am not sure if she knew she was in church. I like to think she has moments of clarity that allow her to enjoy the words of the preacher, like she used to.

It's my job to stay with her through the night. It's not an easy job. She doesn't sleep well most nights. She walks around the house not knowing who she is or where she is. She tries to open the doors and leave home in the middle of the night. I must be on guard throughout the night. Going to class after an exhausting night with Grandmother is trying to say the least.

My grades had begun to suffer, and I missed several days of class. When I *was* able to make it, I was not prepared to be a productive student. My unusual behavior caught the eye of one of my professors. Professor Thomas stopped me after class one day to ask me if everything was okay. He pointed out that there had been a recent decline in the quality of my work.

I explained my situation, and surprisingly he said, "I did not know you were Sister Dottie's granddaughter." He was a member of the same church as my grandmother and asked if there was anything he could do to help. I was grateful for his offer, but I was not a charity case, so I declined. However, Professor Thomas would not take no for an answer. He explained that Sister Dottie was a valued member of his church family and that he wanted to help. He offered me an extension on one assignment, encouraged me to re-do two other assignments and asked for my permission to speak to my other professors about my extenuating circumstances. It was an offer I could not refuse.

It became obvious that church folk talked to one another, because the day after I spoke with Professor Thomas, I received a phone call from Pastor Rawls. His voice was deep and calming. He said he was calling to check on Sister Dottie's progress.

I told him she was doing well. During our conversation, it became apparent that Pastor Rawls really cared about my grandmother and that he had been aware of her illness long before now. He spoke of his many prayer sessions with her when she first became ill. I realized that he had known she was sick long before I did.

He shifted the conversation to my welfare. He wanted to know if I was taking care of myself. It had been a long time since I thought about my own needs. It felt good that someone was concerned about me. I was honest with the pastor and told him that I love my grandmother, but some days were hard. I wished I could wave a magical wand and change everything back to the way it used to be.

The pastor was quiet for a brief moment. Then he cleared his throat and said, "Sister Dottie would not want that."

I was confused. What was he saying? I sat on the phone, silent, with my mouth open in shock.

"Sister Dottie has lived a full life," he continued. "She has no regrets. She is on a journey for the Lord, and there are no short cuts into the Kingdom of the God." He ended the conversation by inviting me to attend church the following Sunday. I told him I would think about it.

After I hung up the phone, I had mixed feelings about the conversation.

On Sunday morning, I decided to go to church. Not because the pastor invited me, but because I knew it would please my grandmother. As we prepared for church, I made sure she put on the yellow dress she loves so much. She asked about wearing her matching hat. I was surprised that she remembered. I placed the hat on her head and pulled the veil down over her face. She smiled at me, and I knew she was having a moment of clarity.

As I drove into the church parking lot, several people paused to wave hello. After I parked the car, two young men came over to assist Grandmother. She stood tall as she walked with a gentleman on each arm. They escorted her up the church steps, and I walked behind, watching her enjoy the moment.

As we entered the church sanctuary, I took her hand, and then we walked down the center aisle. The moment brought back memories, but this time it was different.

We reached the front of the church near the altar, and one of the deacons directed us to the seats on the right side of the pulpit. These seats were normally reserved for the elder saints. I had never sat in the prestigious seats. Ever since I was young, I had referred to this area as the "Amen Corner." I knew I was only allowed to sit there because of my grandmother, but nevertheless, it felt good to be back in church.

The choir began to sing a familiar turn. Grandmother clapped her hands and swayed from side to side in her seat. She was enjoying herself so much that I decided to join in by clapping my hands.

The pastor entered the sanctuary wearing a white robe trimmed in gold. He had his Bible in his right hand and held it clutched to his chest. As he approached the pulpit, he looked in our direction. There was a smile of approval on his face.

The title of his sermon was "Family Unity." He began by saying, "The family unity we share within these church walls must extend outside the church and into our everyday lives." Throughout his sermon, he challenged the church family to take care of each other. His message was well received by the congregation; several people said "Amen" and clapped throughout the service.

At the conclusion of his sermon, he looked at my grandmother and said, "Sister Dottie is a shining example of family dedication." He spoke of her many charitable deeds and her inspiring spirit. Everyone in the church started to clap and stand in her honor. I also rose to my feet to show my appreciation and love for this special woman; my grandmother. The tribute went on for several minutes.

As I gazed around the packed church, I was humbled by the entire experience. Again, I asked myself,

"Who are these people?" But this time, I knew the answer. "This is my family, and I am a part of something special."

My Prayer

Hello, Lord, it's me again. I come to you with a humble heart. I give you all the glory. You have brought me from a long way. I could not have overcome my addiction to crack cocaine without you. My addiction controlled my life. I was running full speed and going nowhere. I have stolen from my family, my friends and complete strangers. I did whatever I had to do to satisfy my habit. I have done so many unspeakable things that I can only share with you, Lord, because others would not understand. You have accepted me and all my indiscretions. I thank you for helping me through the worst time of my life.

You have given my life purpose. I am your humble servant. I joined the church two years ago, and I have served you faithfully. I am a member of the church choir. I never miss a practice rehearsal or a performance. When I sing, I sing with an open heart because I sing in honor of your grace. I attend church service and Sunday school every Sunday without fail except for the one time I was sick with the flu.

Lord, please take notice that I am trying to make amends for my transgressions. I am attempting to rebuild my life for my family and for myself. Everyone is skeptical of my transformation. I understand their skepticism, but they refuse to see the new me. I have been clean for two years, but some people still hold onto the past.

My sister, Marie, is my worst critic. She reminds me often that I am a thief and drug addict. She and I used to be so close, but when I was hooked on 'crack', I stole anything and everything that wasn't nailed down. Marie was one of my favorite target. I stole her silverware that wasn't silver. I stole pieces of her wedding china. I stole figurines off her mantle. I even stole her garden hose. The last straw was when I stole her bankcard and took two hundred dollars out of her account. I would have taken more, but that was the maximum amount the ATM would allow. She cancelled the card after that, and things have not been the same since.

I also betrayed my parents. I stole my dad's carpentry tools from my mom's garage. After my dad's death, my mom stored all his work tools in her garage. I sold them. I sold the tools for little of nothing. I took whatever amount anyone would give me without considering the actual value of the tools. More importantly, I did not consider the sentimental value of the tools and what they meant to my mother. I know my dad was turning over in his grave.

My mother was an easy mark. She wanted to believe that I was just going through a hard time. She would give me money so I would not have to steal or do unspeakable things for money. However, there was never enough, I always needed more. I would take her money and still do whatever I had to for more money and more drugs.

I regret a lot of things that happened during that time of life, but most of all I regret how I let my son down. Jacob was only two years old when my life started to spiral out of control. I don't remember all the details, but I was told I left him home alone for two days. I get sick when I think about it. My neighbor, who was also a 'crack—head,' took Jacob to my mom's house. How could I have put him in such danger? Thank you, God! You were looking over my son when I was unable to take care of him. I know you are still looking over him.

Drugs made me crazy. I tried to bargain with my mom about Jacob's safety. I told her Jacob could stay with her if she gave me one thousand dollars. I threatened to take him away from her if she did not give me the money. I don't think I would have really taken him away, but my mother was not taking any chances. She reported me to the police. She told the police everything. I was arrested for stealing and child abandonment.

At the time, I was in disbelief. How could my mother have me arrested? I did not realize she had done it to save my son from me. Soon after the saga, my mother petitioned the court for custody of my son.

I spent thirty days in jail, where I took part in a detox program, and then I was placed on two years probation. I tried to clean up my act after my brief jail stay. I was determined to do it on my own, without any assistance from anyone. I wanted to show everyone that I was stronger than my habit. However, I wasn't out of jail a month before I went back to my old habits. This time, my addiction was worse than before. I thought I was alone in the world and that 'crack' was my only family and friend.

One night after 'tweekin out' in a crack-house, my heart started to pound extremely fast. I thought it was going to jump out of my chest. I remember falling and hitting the floor. I am not sure how I got to the hospital, but I woke up in the hospital with my mom by my side. She told me I had a heart attack and had been unconscious for two days. The nurse interrupted to say that my mother had been there by my side the entire time. I started to cry. I could not believe that this woman still loved me after all I had done to her. She hugged me and told me we were going to get through this. She said "we." She hadn't given up on me. It had been a long time since I felt loved; I didn't want to let her go.

When I was released from the hospital, I checked myself into the Holy Trinity Rehabilitation Center. The center helped me realize that I needed help to beat my addiction. Several of the employees and volunteers at the center were former addicts; they knew what I was going through. We shared stories and read scriptures from the Bible daily. I had read parts of the Bible before, but this time the meaning was clear and personal. I found strength in believing in your mercy and your power to create miracles. I have been drug-free and devoted my life to you for the last two years.

Lord, I am asking for your continued blessing. I know I don't deserve your goodness and grace, but I am asking to have my son back in my life. I want to do right by him. I want Jacob to see me as his mom and not just the lady who visits every other weekend. I want to bring him home to live with me. My family is not totally convinced of my transformation. I don't want to appear ungrateful for all they have done for Jacob and me, but I am ready to be his mom again. Through your guidance, I have learned patience. I am waiting on your continued deliverance.

Lord, I know I really messed up, and you delivered me beyond my demons. I live to glorify your name, and I will continue to live a Christian life. Thank you for all you have done and all you will do. With these words, I pray. Amen.

Spare the Rod / Spoil the Child

Spare the rod; spoil the child. It's the motto I was raised with. It worked for my sister and me. It worked for my parents and my parents' parents. So when I had my son, Chase, I raised him the same way. I started training Chase when he was a toddler. I taught him early that disobedience would result in punishment. A pop on the hand, a swat on the bottom and an occasional lashing with a belt were my methods of punishment through the years. Chase was a good child; therefore, I didn't have to use corporal punishment often, but when I did it was swift and deliberate. He knew mommy meant business.

By the age thirteen, he knew the rules and he rarely challenged my system. I could not pat myself on the back enough. He was an 'A' student and an aspiring soccer star. My system was working, until the day I received a call from a Ms. McGrady.

Ms. McGrady was a social worker with the Department of Family and Children Services. She asked me to come to her office to discuss some bruises on Chase's legs and back. I was not aware of any bruises.

Chase had received a spanking a few days earlier, but I would never leave bruises on my son. He was punished for lying. Lying is one thing that is unacceptable in my house.

During soccer season, he has practice every Tuesday, Wednesday and Thursday, but because I usually work late on Tuesday his coach would give him a ride home after practice. That week, his Tuesday practice was cancelled; however, no one made me aware of the change. I got off work early that day and wanted to surprise Chase by picking him up from practice. When I got there, the practice field was empty. I was a little concerned, but I assumed practice had ended early and the coach must have taken Chase home. I called my house, but there was no answer. I called his coach, who informed me he had an emergency and practice was cancelled. He instructed all his players to call their parents about the change. The coach apologized for not calling me personally, but Chase told him he had spoken with me and that I was going to pick him up after school. However, I never received a call, so at that moment I had no idea where my child was. That was the most God-awful feeling I ever felt.

I called my house again to see if he was there. He answered the phone. I was relieved but still up-set. My only statement to him was, "We'll talk when I get home." I hung up the phone before he had a chance to say anything.

On the ride home, I talked to myself the entire way. I thanked God for letting him be okay, but the more I thought about him lying, the madder I got. What was he thinking? How did he get home? I could not get home quick enough to get to the bottom of the situation.

Chase was sitting in the living room watching television when I walked in. He said hello in a cheerful voice and asked me how my day was. I told him fine and asked him how practice was. He said, "Good."

My eyes stretched two sizes when I heard his response. He was lying again and to my face. I told him I had gotten off work early and stopped by the soccer field.

His eyes never left the television. He didn't respond. He just sat there like he hadn't heard what I said. I stood in front of the television, and he looked like a deer in the headlights of a car. I grabbed the remote out of his hand and turned the television off. I stared at him for a few seconds without saying a word, and then I said, "Explain yourself."

He started by saying the coach had to leave early; practice was cancelled. He called the team to his office and told everyone to call their parents about the change. Some of the guys decided it would be cool to walk home from school without speaking to their parents, so they told the coach that their parents were coming to pick them up from school. Chase called my old cell phone number that he knew was turned off and pretended to speak with me, leading his coach to think that everything was fine. The lying seemed to come so easy to him.

I was upset about the lying, but I was horrified when I learned he had walked home from the school. I never allowed him to walk home from school because it's a long walk in my opinion and some of streets on the route to our house are known for gang violence. I would have never agreed to him walking home. He was with three other boys, but he lived the farthest away, so he had to walk alone for about three blocks. The situation just kept getting worse. He informed me that the walk home was not a big deal and that he wasn't a baby; he could handle himself.

He put himself in danger and lied to several adults, yet he didn't seem to understand the seriousness of the matter.

It was my job to make sure he understood. I asked him if he knew what integrity meant.

He said, "Kinda."

I went into mommy speech mode. "Having integrity means that you are honest, trustworthy and reliable. Integrity is something you earn that cannot be taken away. You can give it away or throw it away, but no one can take it away. As of today, your integrity was thrown away; I do not trust you. I'm sure your school officials, coaches, and team members will also look at you differently now. You chose to put your wants above everyone else without thinking about what could happen. If something had happened to you or one of the other boys, it would have been devastating for a lot of people. The bottom line is that you lied, Chase, and there is price to be paid for lying."

I sent him to his room and told him I would be there in a minute. I went to my room to get a belt for his punishment. I took no pleasure in spanking him, but it had to be done. I could not just let him think his behavior was acceptable. I said a quick prayer and asked God to let the spanking serve as a deterrent for future misdeeds.

When I entered the room, Chase was laying across his bed. He quickly jumped to his feet. I held the belt in my right hand. It was folded with the buckle in my hand, so I would only hit him with the leather strap part of the belt. I told him to turn around. He knew his butt was the target whenever a spanking was required, but he didn't turn around as usual. He just stood there.

I yelled at him to turn around. He backed up and still refused. I could not believe he was defying me again. I grabbed him by the arm and began to hit him with the belt on his butt. He pulled away from me. I had to chase him around the room. His butt was still the target, but he was moving so much he left me no choice but to hit him wherever I could. The more he ran the more licks he received. He finally caught on and stopped running. The spanking was more intense than I had planned, but when he ran from me, the magnitude of the situation had doubled.

After Ms. McGrady's call, I left work to go to her office as she requested. I had never been to the office of the Department of Family and Children Services. I had to ask someone for directions.

In the lobby of the building, several people were sitting in the waiting area. Their faces looked so sad. I didn't know why they were there, but I know I felt a sense of sadness. I approached the front counter, and the receptionist told me to "Take a number," and then she walked away.

I looked at the number machine. The next number was 42; they were servicing number 29. I didn't take a number. I couldn't wait for a number to be called. I needed to speak with someone quickly. They had called me, and I had to know what was going on with my son. I stood there in front of the counter until she returned.

When she came back, she didn't acknowledge my presence. In a loud voice I said, "Excuse me."

She said, "You need to take a number."

I told her I was Ms. Tate and that I had received a call from Ms. McGrady.

She looked up and said, "Oh, they've been waiting for you." She made a phone call and then directed me to the double doors on the right. She pushed a button; the doors buzzed and opened.

I walked through into a long hallway. A short stocky gentleman in a brown suit was standing in the hall. He called my name and directed me into the third office on the left. Linda McGrady's name was on the door. I assumed she was the lady sitting behind the desk.

The man introduced himself first. He was Officer Randall Smith with Juvenile Services. My assumption was correct: the thin woman behind the desk was Ms. McGrady.

As I looked around the room, I did not see Chase. My first question was, "Where is Chase?"

Officer Smith said he was in an office down the hall with another social worker.

In a condescending tone of voice, Ms. McGrady said, "As I said on the phone earlier, there are some bruises on Chase that we need to discuss with you."

I looked her straight in the eye and said, "What do you need to know? I love my son, and I would do anything for him."

There was obviously tension in the room. Office Smith tried to defuse the situation. He said, "Ms. Tate, I'm sure you love your son, but take a look at these pictures." He gave me his cell phone and showed me five pictures. They were pictures of Chase. I went through the pictures a couple of times to make sure. Chase has a birthmark on his back, and the person in the picture had the same mark. There were two pictures of his legs, two pictures of his back and one picture of his right arm. Each picture showed light red marks on the body parts.

When I looked up after viewing the pictures, Ms. McGrady said, "Would you like to add anything to your previous statement?"

I said, "Yes. The light red marks on these pictures are barely noticeable. In your phone call you said bruises like he was black and blue."

Officer Smith quickly stepped in again by saying they had already spoken to Chase, but they needed to hear from me what happened.

I turned to speak directly to the officer, ignoring Ms. McGrady. I told him about the recent spanking and the reason behind the punishment.

Ms. McGrady interrupted and added her two cents. She said, "Whenever you leave marks on a child in the name of punishment, you have gone too far." This time the officer did not intervene. He let her have the floor. She continued by saying that from their conversation with Chase, they did not believe I had intentionally hurt him, but nevertheless the result was the same.

Regardless of her tone, she was right. She leaned over her desk, extending her hand to give me a card with the dates and times of upcoming parent support groups. I accepted the card, although I did not plan to attend a support group. I asked to see Chase. They both agreed to my request.

When Officer Smith left the room to get my son, Ms. McGrady had to have the last word: "Ms. Tate, I am not your enemy. My number is at the bottom of the card I gave you. My job is to help families, and right now your family is in need. If you need any assistance, don't hesitate to give me a call."

I did not respond.

The officer returned with Chase. Chase came over to where I was sitting without being instructed and stood beside me. Speaking to the both of us, Officer Smith said that parents have the right to disciple their children, but they do not have the right to cause physical harm or leave marks of any kind. He told Chase that in the future he must follow the rules of the house. He strongly suggested that I take advantage of the parent support group. He also said the incident would go on record and that his office would be in touch to check on our progress.

Chase and I left the office together. The ride home was solemn. Chase spoke first. He said he had not told anyone about the spanking, but when he was changing for soccer practice a couple of his teammates noticed the marks and told their coach, and the coach had filed the report. His voice was trembling as he spoke. He clutched the passenger door during the entire ride home.

I told him that I wasn't angry, but I didn't want to talk at that moment. My mind was spinning a mile a minute. How could anyone accuse me of abusing my child? He had faint, light-red marks not bruises. Chase knew I loved him and would do anything for him.

When we arrived home, Chase went to his room, and I went to mine. I was mentally drained. I got in my bed and pulled the cover over my head. Ms. McGrady's words stayed in my head: "Whenever you leave marks on a child in the name of punishment, you have gone too far. Whenever you leave marks on a child in the name of punishment, you have gone too far. You have gone too far." Did I go too far?

'Spare the rod; spoil the child': I had lived by these words all my life. What did the words truly mean? Were my parents wrong? Was I wrong? Was I using the words as justification for what I did? That was not the first time I had left red marks on my child. The bruises were real, and it was my fault. Earlier, I had told Ms. McGrady that I loved my son and would do anything for him. I asked God to forgive me for hurting Chase and to help me be a better parent. I emerged from the covers with a new perspective.

I knocked on Chase's bedroom door and waited for him to invite me in. When I entered the room, he was sitting at his desk. I held out my arms for a hug. He walked over and gave me a hug. As we embraced, I told him I was sorry. He also apologized. We talked for about an hour and agreed that we both had some things we needed to work on.

The next day, I called Ms. McGrady to inquire about the parent support group. 'Spare the rod; spoil the child': is still my motto, but now my rod is not a belt.

Thanks for Sending an Angel

When I got married, there was no doubt in my mind that Malcolm and I would be together forever. We met in college. I was a freshman, and he was a senior. I was sitting alone at a table in the library when he asked if he could sit with me. We talked for hours. Neither one of us did much studying that day. Soon after that, we became a couple. Every time he introduced me as his girlfriend, I blushed with pleasure. I was a freshman, and my boyfriend was a senior, about to graduate. All of my friends were envious. They wanted to know if he had any brothers like him at home. No such luck. He was an only child, and he was mine.

The summer after my freshman year of college, I found out I was pregnant. I was happy and scared at the same time. I was happy that I was going to have a baby with Malcolm, but I was scared because I wasn't sure how he was going to react to the news. I knew he loved me, but a baby wasn't in the plan. The plan was for him to go to law school and for me to go back to college for my sophomore year. My pregnancy wasn't supposed to happen until we were both finished school, and our careers were well established. The plan changed.

When I told Malcolm I was pregnant, he was very excited. He hugged and kissed me several times. His reaction was more intense than I could have imaged. He was so happy; his eyes filled with tears and one teardrop ran down his face. He touched my stomach repeatedly. He talked to my stomach like he was talking directly to the baby. He referred to the baby as he. He was hoping for a boy.

I could not have asked for a better reaction, or so I thought. He sat down beside me on the couch and said, "Let's get married." It wasn't the proposal I had dreamt about. I had imagined him on one knee in a black tux, holding a tiny black-velvet box with a large diamond ring inside it. I would say, "Yes," and then he would place the ring on my finger with a kiss, sealing our bond. But considering the circumstances, I was grateful he asked. He didn't have to ask me twice. I said yes.

The next step was to tell our parents. We spoke to my parents first. Initially, we didn't tell them I was pregnant; we just said we were getting married. My mom grabbed my hand and asked to see the ring. I didn't have a ring at that time, but before I could explain she looked in my eyes, still holding my hand and said, "You're pregnant."

I was relieved I didn't have to speak the words. I didn't want her to be disappointed in me. She took the news better than I thought. She smiled and turned to my father and said, "We are going to be grandparents."

My dad gave his nod of approval. He shook Malcolm's hand and said, "Congratulations."

Malcolm's parents were not so happy. His father was furious. He called Malcolm irresponsible and wanted to know how he could let this happen.

Malcolm fired back and said, "I didn't come here for your permission or your approval. I came here as a courtesy."

His dad insisted that the two of them speak alone in the study. His mother and I remained in the family room. She was less vocal and only said, "My son must really love you. He has never challenged his father like this before."

Malcolm emerged from the study alone. He took my hand, and we quickly walked out the front door.

His parents eventually gave us their blessings. We were married five weeks after his proposal. We accomplished a lot in that short time. We secured the church and reception hall, sent invitations, hired a band and purchased a wedding dress. The wedding occurred without a hitch. We were married in the church where I grew up. We wrote our own vows for the ceremony. When he spoke of his love for me, it was as if I could see straight into his heart. I could not have asked for a better wedding day. We were surrounded with family and friends, and everyone had a great time.

After the wedding, we had to come up with some new plans for our future. We moved in with my parents until we could find a suitable place we could afford. With a baby on the way, I couldn't go back to school, and I couldn't work either because I was extremely sick during my pregnancy. Malcolm decided to put law school on hold and got a job teaching history at a local high school. It wasn't ideal, but we made it work.

After five months, we moved into our own apartment and two months later Emily was born. She was the most beautiful baby I had ever seen. My instant love for her was like nothing I had ever felt. Her father was obsessed with her happiness and with securing her future. He took a second job as a security guard to make additional money. I went to work part-time as a cashier at a drug store. We never made a move without considering Emily's welfare.

Parenthood is not easy. Malcolm and I struggled to balance parenthood and marriage. We focused so much on Emily's happiness that we neglected each other.

By the time Emily started the terrible twos, Malcolm and I could barely stand to be in the same room. Somewhere along the way we stopped communicating with each other. We would only talk about Emily or things related to her. She was the subject of all our conversations. We pretended for a long time that everything was fine, but it wasn't. We went from not speaking to each other to yelling at each other. It was bad.

We tried marriage counseling, but things seemed to get worse not better. Counseling helped me see that I was no longer the shy young girl Malcolm had married. I felt controlled and confined in the marriage. The more I tried to express my feelings the more we argued.

The day finally came when the 'D' word was spoken. We were having one of our usual arguments when I said, "I want a divorce." He became angrier than I had ever seen him before. He broke the mirror in the bedroom with his fist. Luckily, Emily was with my mother and missed this argument, although she had been present for most of the others.

He moved out, while Emily and I remained in the apartment. My parents wanted us to move back in with them, but that would have been like taking one step forward and two steps backwards. Malcolm didn't waste any time serving me with the divorce papers; they arrived two weeks after he moved out. He was trying to control the situation, but I wasn't going to let that happen. I didn't agree to his terms, and I wasn't going to let him have his way.

We went back and forth for months before we agreed on custody, child support, visitations, vacations, holidays, insurance, and previous financial obligations. When the divorce was final, I never expected for Malcolm and me to be close friends. I had hoped we would be civil to each other for Emily's sake. However, Malcolm was not interested in having any kind of relationship with me. On his visitation days, he made arrangements for his mother to pick up Emily so he would not have to see me. The situation was far from perfect, but Emily loved her dad and he loved her.

We had been divorced for over a year when my life started to change for the better. I was promoted to manager at the drug store. I enrolled in a night class at the local community college. I felt good about myself. I even went out on a couple of dates. I was happy and exploring my options.

Malcolm heard about my new endeavors, and he wasn't happy. He hadn't spoken to me since the divorce, but he called me out of the blue to tell me I was bad mother. He said I worked too many hours and complained that I allowed strange men around his daughter. His calls became more frequent and brutal. He complained about everything. In his eyes, I could not do anything right. His threat to take Emily away from me was his biggest weapon.

I wasn't innocent in the verbal exchange; my words were just a vicious. I made sure he knew I had ways of controlling his visitations with Emily. She might have a cold on his next visitation day and have to stay home. His biggest fear was that I would turn Emily against him, and I used it to my advantage. We were arguing like we had when we were married. It was bad all over again.

Then all of a sudden, he changed. He was nice. He apologized for all the mean things he had said and done. I was skeptical. I didn't know what he was up to, but I was going to enjoy it while it lasted. Suddenly we were able to have a conversation without criticizing each other or yelling. I wasn't surprised to learn that a woman was the inspiration behind his change. He met Allison through a friend. She asked him to go to church with her and he agreed. In the beginning, he went to church just to be close to her, but the more he went the more he enjoyed the spiritual lessons and the people. It was the therapy he needed to get over his anger and move on with his life.

As a young boy, Malcolm attended a private Christian school. He was an usher in his church by age ten. His mother and father still attended the church where he was baptized. When Malcolm went to college, he stopped going to church and his faith seemed to waiver.

Allison reintroduced Malcolm to his faith. She pointed him in the right direction, and he followed his heart the rest of the way. They are couple now, and I wish them well. Their personalities are a perfect fit for one another. He can be strong willed and opinionated while she is more flexible and open-minded. Their relationship has grown along with their faith. I have not seen Malcolm this happy and at peace for years. He is really trying to be a better person and father.

Our relationship as a couple didn't work, but we are working together to be better parents for Emily. Allison came into our lives at the perfect time. She is a welcome addition to our family. Angels come in all forms.

Sanctuary

Last week, I ran into one of my church members at the mall. That was the first time I had seen her in many months. I think she saw me before I saw her. She was navigating through the food-court crowd in the opposite direction of my location. I yelled her name: "Marina!"

She didn't turn around or stop. She kept walking. I thought maybe she didn't hear my first call, so I yelled a little louder, and then several more times. I think she thought if she made a few extra turns and walked really fast, she would stay clear of my path. But she was wrong; I followed her, calling her name, until she had no choice but to stop.

She said, "Hello Pastor Norton."

Jokingly, I said, "You do remember my name." We embraced with a light hug. It was good to see her. I asked about her welfare and inquired about her family. I was happy to hear that she and her family were doing well.

I asked her if she was going to a new church. To my surprise, she said she wasn't going to a new church or any church. Her explanation for not attending church was one that I hear time and time again. Her work schedule had changed and she was required to work on Sunday.

I told her that I understood, but I reminded her about Wednesday Night Bible Study and our many other church functions.

She smiled and said, "Pastor, I don't have a valid excuse for missing church. I missed one Sunday and then another. The next thing I knew, I had stopped going to church altogether."

I asked her if she had a minute to sit and speak with me. She looked at her watch and said she really had to go. I was disappointed by her response. I told her I understood and I hoped it wouldn't be months before I see her again.

She sighed and lowered her head. She mumbled, "I think I can spare a few minutes."

We walked to one of the nearby vacant tables in the food court area.

She started the conversation by saying, "I am a good person. I don't wish anyone ill will. I do what I can to help my fellow man. I say my prayers every day, and I read my Bible often. I don't read it as often as I should, but that's between me and God. I'm not perfect, but no one is perfect. And, besides half the people in the church are sinners anyway. How can they help me when they can't help themselves?" She didn't stop there. She went on to say, "I don't have to be inside a church for God to hear my prayers. I don't just pray for myself; I pray for others as well. I know in my heart that God is watching over me, even if I am not inside the church walls. Isn't God everywhere?"

I was about to respond, but she wasn't finished.

"Pastor, I will give you credit I enjoyed listening to your sermons most of the time, but sometimes you rambled on a little too much for me. I think I get what I need from reading the Bible and from saying my prayers."

Her comments were enlightening. It was my turn to speak. I had to choose my words carefully, because apparently I tend to ramble. "The church is more than just a building, the members are more than just people and prayers are more than just words. You are right. God is everywhere. But that's not the issue. You said it yourself: no one is perfect. Living a Christian life can be difficult at times. The world is filled with obstacles that are intent on blocking our path to the Promised Land. You don't have to travel your path alone. Our congregation is made up of a lot of good people. They are not perfect, but who is? We all need assistance from time to time, and that is when you call on your fellow church members. Or maybe that is when someone calls on you."

She started to bite her bottom lip as I was speaking. I took that as a cue that I was rambling, but I had a few more things to say. I tried to be brief. "The church is a sanctuary. Sanctuary means safe haven. The freedom to worship with people who believe as you do can be very powerful. It's like electricity in the air. I and many others, draw strength from worshiping with family and friends in the Sanctuary. The love in the Sanctuary is what makes it so special; it's not the building."

"Individual worship is a very personal thing and apparently you have made your choice. I commend you for continuing to worship in spite of not attending church services. But whenever you are ready to come back to church, we will welcome you with open arms."

She smiled and said, "Thank you." We both stood up to leave. We embraced again. As we hugged, I said, "I hope I didn't ramble."

GOD is....

Reverend Robert Warren became the pastor of our church six months ago, after Pastor Sullivan retired.

Pastor Sullivan was the leader of Greater Valley Mission Church for twenty-seven years. I have known him my entire life. He baptized me when I was just a little girl. I wasn't afraid of the water, because I trusted him. Pastor Sullivan is truly a Godly man. He doesn't just speak the words of God; he lives by them every day. A few members thought his leadership style was a little rigid. He made it a point to have an agenda for every church service, Bible study group and meeting. He rarely deviated from the agenda. I liked his style. There were no surprises; I knew what to expect and that gave me comfort. He was the pastor of our congregation for a long time. Change will not come easy.

Reverend Warren has really shaken things up in our church. Reverend Bob, as he likes to be called, is a different kind of minister. He says he's thirty-four years old, but he looks like he's barely twenty-one. He stands about five feet ten inches. He weighs about 150 pounds soaking wet. His southern drawl reminds me of Andy Taylor from the Andy Griffith Show. He even looks a little like Andy Taylor.

He's always trying new things. The first thing he changed was the format of Sunday Programs. Not everyone was happy with the removal of two choir selections, but so far so good. He even changed Wednesday Bible Study from seven o'clock to six o'clock. That caused a few rumblings in the church, but more people seem to attend now than before.

Last Wednesday night at Bible Study, he gave everyone a pencil and a sheet of paper. At the top of the page were the words "God is...." He told the group not to speak to each other until he had an opportunity to explain the lesson. Once everyone was seated, he explained that he wanted everyone to complete the statement at the top of the page. He wanted everyone to give his or her own individual thoughts without worrying about spelling, punctuation or word count; he wanted everyone to express what was in their hearts. He gave us ten minutes to write.

I thought to myself, Wow, this is different. I was so used to someone telling me what to believe and think that I was having difficulty deciding what to write. Reverend Bob would speak occasionally, saying, "Write what is in your heart." My mind was blank. God is...I sat there for a few more minutes with nothing on my page. I felt like I was taking a pop quiz that I was unprepared for. Time was running out. In a panic, I wrote "Love." God is Love. Time was called. I just hoped Rev. Bob would not call on me to share.

He asked for volunteers to share what they wrote. Several people raised their hands. A few people said the same thing I said; God is Love. Others said, God is my Shepard; God is All knowing; God is Forgiving; God is Everywhere; plus many others. A few of the comments stood out more than others. Ms. Tammy was usually shy and quiet, but that day she stood up and read her comments loud and proud. "God is amazing. Every day I wake up to a new day, I am always amazed that God has blessed me with the miracle of life. The longer I live, the more I appreciate all his gifts. I don't want to waste a minute of my life because God has judged me worthy of his blessing."

Syren is only seventeen, but she spoke like a grownup that day. She said, "God is always with me. I know most grownups think teenagers are selfish, lazy and insensitive. I am guilty of all those things at one time or another. The pressure of being a teenager is very real, and the pressure of being a teenage girl is even more intense. I am forced to make decisions every day that will affect the rest of my life. I have made some mistakes, and I'm sure I'll make plenty more. I am learning to be a good Christian. It's not easy, but through it all I know God is always with me."

Mr. Johnson's words were the most moving. He used his cane to slowly rise to his feet. He stood with his left hand on his cane and his paper in his right hand. Standing wasn't a requirement; I guess he just wanted to stand as the others had done. In his slow monotone voice he said, "God is not always fair." A low gasp could be heard in the church. Mr. Johnson continued, "I know people think I'm crazy for saying that, but that's how I feel. As most of you know, several months ago a drunk driver hit, my wife, Lilly and me as we were driving home from a restaurant. My leg was broken in three places and my collarbone was also broken. I was in the hospital for three days. My Lilly was not so lucky."

His voice cracked. He stopped reading from his paper. He was speaking from his heart. He said, "Lilly was pronounced dead at the scene of the accident. One moment we were celebrating our twenty-first anniversary, and the next moment I was making funeral arrangements. The most troubling part of it all is that the drunk driver walked away from the accident with just a few scratches. No broken bones, no hospital stay, no nothing. And right now he's out on bail, walking around and living his life like nothing has happened. I am struggling to understand why and how God would let this happen." At the end of his statement, he slowly sat back in his seat and wiped his eyes with his white handkerchief. Several other people were also wiping their eyes.

The church was silent. Reverend Bob stood up in front of the Bible Study Group and thanked everyone who shared their statements. He stood there for a brief moment with his hands in his pockets without saying a word. I think he was caught off-guard by Mr. Johnson's emotional response. He took a deep breath and said, "I must say this exercise has been very enlightening for all us today. Today I decided to try something a little different. Normally you come to hear me speak the word of God, but today I wanted to know what you had to say. I wanted to know your ideas, your feelings, your wants and your desires. When you walked in, I told you not to talk to anyone about the lesson. I wanted you to write down your own thoughts. I didn't want anyone to be swayed by the ideas others. All too often we rely on others to tell us how we should feel and what we should think.

"As your pastor, it's my job to help you interpret the scriptures, Bible verses and meaning of God's will. My job is to help. I don't ever want anyone to follow me blindly or agree with my every word because I am your pastor. I want you to think for yourselves and share your ideas with me and with each other. We can all learn from one another. I am encouraged by today's lesson. You all had some interesting things to say today. I was inspired and moved."

"Speaking from the heart can be very difficult for some people. The heart is a very complicated and fragile organ, both figuratively and literally. Sometimes the heart is filled with joy and happiness. Sometimes it's filled with pain and sorrow. If you are blessed to have joy and happiness in your heart, treasure it and work at keeping it there. Joy and happiness doesn't happen by accident. You work at it by being diligent to God's word and living a Christian lifestyle. If you have pain and sorrow in your heart, know that you are not being punished. Sometimes God's plans are not obvious to us, but take comfort in knowing there is always a reason for his will."

"This exercise showed our differences while highlighting our common bond. The fact that all of you took time out of your busy schedules to come to Wednesday Night Bible Study shows that your faith in God is strong. Our daily lives are all different; we are faced with different challenges. Whether you are married or single, happy or sad, gainfully employed or struggling financially, your presence here is greatly appreciated and needed. Everyone's life and experiences have value. We can learn from each other and help one another."

By the end of his speech, I knew what I wanted to write. I started to write; the words seemed to flow from my pencil. Rev. Bob has really shaken up our church, but sometimes change is good.

What's Your Story?

_____

_____

_____

_____

_____

_____

_____

_____

_____

_____

_____

_____

_____

_____

_____

_____

_____

_____

_____

_____

Made in the USA
Charleston, SC
05 October 2011